$20.95

6/29/16

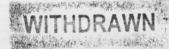

Case of the Sabotaged Spaghetti

By J.L. Anderson
Illustrated by David Ouro

Rourke
Educational Media
rourkeeducationalmedia.com

www.rourkeeducationalmedia.com

Edited by: Keli Sipperley
Cover and Interior layout by: Jen Thomas
Cover and Interior Illustrations by: David Ouro

Library of Congress PCN Data

Case of the Sabotaged Spaghetti / J.L. Anderson
 (Rourke's Mystery Chapter Books)
 ISBN (hard cover)(alk. paper) 978-1-63430-384-2
 ISBN (soft cover) 978-1-63430-484-9
 ISBN (e-Book) 978-1-63430-579-2
 Library of Congress Control Number: 2015933740

Printed in the United States of America, North Mankato, Minnesota

Dear Parents and Teachers:

With twists and turns and red herrings, readers will enjoy the challenge of Rourke's Mystery Chapter Books. This series set at Watson Elementary School builds a cast of characters that readers quickly feel connected to. Embedded in each mystery are experiences that readers encounter at home or school. Topics of friendship, family, and growing up are featured within each book.

Mysteries open many doors for young readers and turn them into lifelong readers because they can't wait to find out what happens next. Readers build comprehension strategies by searching out clues through close reading in order to solve the mystery.

This genre spreads across many areas of study including history, science, and math. Exploring these topics through mysteries is a great way to engage readers in another area of interest. Reading mysteries relies on looking for patterns and decoding clues that help in learning math skills.

Whether readers are reading the books independently or you are reading with them, engaging with them after they have read the book is still important. We've included several activities at the end of each book to make this both fun and educational.

Do you think you and your reader have what it takes to be a detective? Can you solve the mystery? Will you accept the challenge?

Rourke Educational Media

Table of Contents

Chapter One

Surprise!

Klaude liked jokes more than surprises. Jokes made people laugh, most of the time. Surprises weren't always fun and they weren't always good. Plus, there was usually a long, drawn out wait to find out about the surprise, not to mention the surprise almost never included Klaude.

That's exactly how Klaude felt now as Mrs. Holmes gave a long speech during morning assembly about a new surprise at Watson Elementary School—a Golden Spoon Award for excellent lunchroom behavior. "Another surprise includes a Good Manners Luncheon for the award winners and their families," she said.

"Boring," Klaude said under his breath, even though a spaghetti dinner at the Good Manners Luncheon plus cake for dessert didn't sound all that boring.

A girl named Divya said and gave him a dirty look. "Shh!" Everyone at Watson knew she thought Klaude was annoying. She whispered something to her friend who was a good artist. This gave Klaude an idea to help pass the time in morning assembly.

He doodled a picture of two meatballs on a scrap sheet of paper while Mrs. Holmes spoke. This Golden Spoon Award thing didn't concern him. Like any of the teachers or the cafeteria workers would've picked me for the award, he thought. Sometimes people took Klaude's jokes the wrong way and a few of the teachers at Watson considered Klaude a troublemaker. It didn't matter if he always said thank you or cleaned up or volunteered. He even helped Nurse Strongman out at the health fair recently.

Klaude ripped the paper meatballs off of the page and placed the scraps over his eyes. He groaned like a zombie, but not so loud his teacher, Mr. Hambrick, could hear.

Mrs. Holmes called out a few names and then said, "Klaude." This was followed by the group clapping.

Klaude still had a paper meatball over his left eye when he looked up. "Huh?"

Lots of the third graders laughed. Klaude wasn't even trying to be funny. The meatball doodle fell off of his face and he slipped it in his pocket.

Mrs. Holmes gave him a look down her nose that Klaude and the other kids called the Holmes Eye. "Come talk to me after assembly for more details," Mrs. Holmes said.

More details? Klaude had no clue what was going on. He had a feeling he was about to get in trouble, so it surprised him when Divya said, "I'm shocked. Congratulations."

Klaude had no idea what she was talking about. "Gesundheit," he said. Divya gave him a funny look.

Klaude started to explain to Divya that "gesundheit" was a German word for saying good health after a sneeze, but then she stopped him. "I know what it means, I just don't know why you said it to me."

Divya moved on and then Romy elbowed Klaude as they started making their way out of the cafeteria. "I should've won the Golden Spoon Award, not you. I might've if you hadn't dared me to see how far I could throw my roll. I never meant to start a food fight."

"I never made you do you anything," Klaude said, remembering the messy food fight. After Klaude's dare, Romy threw a buttery roll across the table and accidentally hit a girl named Veronica against her back. Veronica threw her container of applesauce back at Romy, only it was slightly open. It showered applesauce over a bunch of kids. After that, everyone went crazy throwing stuff and the cafeteria staff had to jump in piles of food to get the kids to stop. Klaude had never seen

Mrs. Holmes so upset.

"When are you going to let it go, Romy?" Klaude asked.

"Probably not for a while, especially since you got picked for the Golden Spoon Award. You of all people!" Romy said.

Had Klaude actually won the Golden Spoon Award, or was Romy just teasing him? Divya wasn't the type to tease—why else would she have said congratulations?

Several other kids were talking to Mrs. Holmes after the assembly and Klaude could hardly stand still.

"Are you doing the potty dance?" Veronica asked him. Mrs. Holmes must've called her name too.

"Funny," Klaude said and forced himself to stand still even if he was super anxious to find out more about why Mrs. Holmes wanted to talk to him.

When it was Klaude's turn to talk to Mrs. Holmes, she smiled at him. The principal reminded him of his grandmother, only a smaller version. Mrs. Holmes' clothes were much nicer than what Klaude's grandmother, Oma, had. They didn't have much money and Oma hadn't bought any new clothes in a while.

"Since you were having an issue with your eyes," Mrs. Holmes said, "you might not have heard the announcement that you won the Golden Spoon Award for a new category, Most Improved Behavior. We look forward to celebrating with you and your family at the luncheon."

No joke, Klaude had won a Golden Spoon Award! He couldn't wait to invite Oma to the luncheon—his only family member. Maybe he needed to give surprises more credit.

Chapter Two

Dancing, Guesses, Music, and a Shriek

"Oma! Guess what?" Klaude said when he came home. Oma's apartment was small and bright as she kept every window open. They didn't own any pets, although Oma had plenty of potted plants all over the place that Oma said were like family members.

Klaude closed the front blinds for privacy. Oma was dressed up in a bright orange leotard and she practiced her dance moves with a plant, a peace lily. She'd been a dancer back in the day, but Klaude didn't need everyone in the apartment complex to see what was going on.

Oma kept right on dancing with the lily as she tried to guess Klaude's news. "The president called because he knows you're a genius and wants you to become an international spy?"

Klaude shook his head. The students at Watson

loved solving mysteries, but no way would any of them become international spies. Well, probably not anyway. "Guess again." Klaude didn't think his grandmother would be able to guess that he won an award, not in a million years, but this was a fun game to play. Oma liked to joke, maybe even more than Klaude.

"You met Peter Rabbit on the bus ride home?" Oma asked. She twirled and then dipped the potted lily. The plant hung down like a head of weird thick green hair. Klaude wondered if plants got motion sick. If so, this plant was doomed. Klaude doubted the motion sickness thing though because Oma's grew so green and healthy.

Klaude shook his head no. Oma made a couple more guesses about Klaude's news: he followed a leprechaun and found the pot of gold, he figured out how to time travel, or maybe he met a Martian at school today. No one could make Klaude laugh quite like his grandmother.

Oma was out of breath. She set the lily down before stretching. "Last guess ... you won an important award and we're going to a fancy lunch together?"

Klaude couldn't believe she knew this whole time! "How did you find out?"

"Mr. Hambrick was so proud of you that he called me to brag about my genius of a grandson," Oma said, smiling at him.

When had a teacher ever called to brag about him before? Oma's eyes lit up with pride and he wanted his grandmother to always look at him that way.

"We'll buy something special to wear for the luncheon," Oma said.

"But what about the cost of new clothes?" Klaude asked, helping himself to a tangerine almost the same color as his grandmother's leotard.

"I have some money set aside for a special occasion, and this my dear boy, is a special occasion."

"One small request," Klaude said.

"Anything for you," Oma replied. Since Klaude's parents had died in an accident when he was a baby, his grandmother always did the best she could to take care of him.

"Can you wear something other than an orange leotard?"

"Be careful what you wish for," Oma said and cackled.

Klaude wasn't sure whether to laugh or worry. He picked up his favorite thing that used to belong to his mom, a wooden recorder, and played a song. Oma started dancing all over again, and Klaude played music until his grandmother grabbed him to dance a polka.

******

Time seemed to drag before the Good Manners Luncheon and then it was suddenly here. Oma helped him slick his wavy hair back and picked out a nice black polo with tan dress pants.

Klaude had expected the worse for Oma's outfit, but she looked tall and beautiful in a traditional German-styled dress. Klaude looked at pictures of his mother often and could see the resemblance between her and Oma. "You look nice, Oma."

"You're growing up to be a fine young man," Oma said. "Your parents would be so proud of you."

The cafeteria looked fancy. The long tables were decorated with white tablecloths and black napkins, the school colors. The best decorations were the homemade trophies displaying a painted golden spoon with each student's name on it. Only Klaude couldn't find his. Maybe the kid who won "Most Improved Behavior" didn't get a golden spoon trophy.

"Whoa, who are you and what did you do with Klaude?" a girl named Queeneka said when she saw him. She was one of the award winners too. She wore a frilly dress fit for a TV award show rather than for a Golden Spoon Award ceremony in the school cafeteria.

The luncheon was crowded with the ten award winners from various grades and all of their families. Several young kids were there, including Bennett's much younger brother, Bradyn, who ran around and weaved through Klaude's legs.

"You were just like that as a little kid," Oma said. "I should let his father borrow the leash I used to control you," Oma whispered to Klaude. When they sat down, Oma cried out in pain.

"Are you okay?" Klaude asked.

"Fine," she said and then moved something out of the way.

Klaude figured she'd been overdoing the dancing lately. Several third graders, including

Divya, volunteered at the luncheon to serve the food and help the cafeteria staff. Romy was there and he stuck out his tongue at Klaude. Klaude crossed his eyes at him and stuck out his tongue in return.

Just then he got the Holmes Eye when the principal welcomed the group and congratulated them before the volunteers passed out the food. Klaude didn't feel deserving of any award, whether or not he got a trophy.

Klaude was determined to be on his best behavior from then on. But he shrieked only a moment later when he took a bite of spaghetti!

Chapter Three

Mayhem

The first bite of spaghetti was delicious. He could tell the noodles had been cooked just right. It might've been a Good Manners Luncheon, but he took an extra-large bite the second time. His mouth was full and then his tooth hit something

hard. There was no way the spaghetti was that hard.

He pulled out a small snake and let out a scream.

Then Queekeka shrieked when she watched him inspect the snake. The snake was only a small plastic toy. Realistic, yes, but harmless.

Veronica cried out, "Eww! You're disgusting, Klaude!" Several of the other volunteers freaked out and Klaude heard whispers that he should've never been picked for a Golden Spoon Award. Bradyn went wild with laughter as he ran over to see the snake. Romy was laughing, too.

"Is there a problem?" Mrs. Holmes asked.

Even his grandmother was staring at him in disbelief. "Why are you causing mayhem?"

Klaude's face burned hot and his stomach churned. "I didn't do anything! Someone put the toy snake in my food."

Several other people gasped and gathered around Klaude's plate of food to see the snake. Bennett looked worried and then chased after Bradyn as he started running laps all over the cafeteria. Their father joined in on the chase.

Bradyn even ran behind the food counters, which was a real health no-no.

"I'll make sure you get a new plate of food," Mrs. Holmes said to Klaude. "We'll get to the bottom of what happened."

Klaude sure hoped so. Who would've put a snake in his spaghetti and why? He already had a suspect, a rather wild one in mind. He put the snake on a napkin and planned on washing it off to keep.

******

Divya walked over with a new plate of spaghetti for Klaude, only Bradyn bumped into her as he ran wild again. Divya's balance was already off

because she walked with ankle braces. Just as Oma tried to help steady her, Divya fell over and dropped spaghetti all over Klaude's new outfit.

Klaude had never owned something as nice as the black polo shirt and the tan dress pants. Now his clothes might've been ruined. All of the award winners and volunteers laughed at him. He wanted to scream, and Divya looked like she was about to start crying. Jokes came in handy at times like this. Klaude helped Divya up and then he clapped. Spaghetti rolled off of his clothes and plopped on the ground. "I give this performance a perfect ten!"

No one said anything. They weren't sure what to make of Klaude's joke. Oma helped save the awkward moment by clapping. Then Queeneka clapped and so did everyone else.

Bennett's father made Bradyn come over to Divya and Klaude to apologize. Queeneka helped Divya out and said she had another dress that she could borrow. Of course a girl like Queeneka came prepared with several dresses, and it was no surprise to Klaude as to why she won an award for good behavior.

Klaude wanted to think of a funny joke to help lighten the mood, only this was a good time to talk to the suspect. "Why did you put a snake in my food?" he asked the little boy.

Bennett gave Klaude a serious look. "My little brother didn't do anything."

"It was funny," Bradyn said, wiping off something pink or red from his face with the back of his hand. Then the little boy pretended he was Klaude and acted out the whole snake scene. Klaude's face burned hot again.

"What a great actor you are," Oma said.

"So, did you do it?" Klaude asked the little boy. He shook his head. "No."

"C'mon," Bennett said to his little brother, "we better finish eating our lunch. Cake is coming soon and you won't get any unless you calm down."

Bradyn laughed and then bolted back to the table.

"I'm worried what that boy will be like once he eats all that sugar," Oma said. She helped Klaude pick up the spaghetti mess on the floor and several of the volunteers did too, including Romy.

"Looks like you started a mini food fight,"

Romy said with a smirk.

Klaude wanted to have a chat with him, but now wasn't the time. Klaude went to the bathroom to wash his hands and his clothes the best he could, and when he returned, he saw that there indeed was a golden spoon trophy with his name on it sitting on the table, only it was broken in half!

Chapter Four

Taking a Bite out of the Mystery

Oma had won a few trophies for dancing by the time she was Klaude's age, and sadly, this was Klaude's first trophy. Maybe it might be his only trophy in his entire life. And now it was broken in half. Why did someone do this to him? Had Klaude hurt someone's feelings by joking? Was someone trying to play a joke on him? If so, how mean!

Oma must've sensed Klaude was upset because she gave him a hug, not caring if her nice dress got dirty. "I'm sorry. Superglue and Oma will come to the rescue later," she said with a smile.

Sure, the trophy might get fixed, but it would always look broken to him. And this luncheon wasn't turning out to be the wonderful event he wanted it to be. Some surprise.

BURP!

Klaude turned around as Bradyn burped a couple more times. Mrs. Holmes looked over as well and she must've given him the Holmes Eye because he said, "Oopsie!" Bennett had his hands over his face like he was embarrassed. They were at a Good Manners Luncheon after all. Sometimes Klaude wished he had a little brother or sister, but other times, like now, he was glad to be an only child.

Bradyn said he didn't put the snake in his spaghetti, if he was telling the truth. It was possible he'd done something to the trophy. He was running wild all over the place and could've played around with it or dropped it by accident. Klaude thought of Romy's smirk as well. He sure seemed guilty and had more reason than Bradyn to mess with his things.

Klaude was just about to excuse himself to talk to Romy and Bradyn when the volunteers started serving slices of cake on fancy gold paper plates. This luncheon suddenly improved, he thought.

Divya, now wearing Queeneka's frilly dress, passed Klaude a thick slice of white cake with at least half an inch of strawberry frosting. He couldn't wait to eat it, but just as he was about to dig his fork into the frosting, he noticed someone had already taken a bite out of his cake!

Maybe he was mistaken—it could've just been an odd knife mark when someone cut the cake. Klaude studied the missing chunk of his cake closer, hoping his first thought was wrong. He doubted a knife or a serving utensil would've looked just like front teeth, though. The teeth marks looked small, at least smaller than an adult's set of teeth. The right front tooth bite mark was clear though the left front tooth looked different—less defined.

"Oma, will you do me a favor?" Klaude whispered. She was just about to sink her fork into her cake. Neither one of them ate cake very often because Oma said it wasn't part of a dancer's diet. Not that Klaude considered himself much of a dancer.

"Anything for you, Klaude," Oma said.

"Will you bite into your cake with your teeth instead of your fork?" Klaude asked.

Other grandmothers might've looked at him funny or asked him why or told him no, but not Oma. "This reminds me of being a little girl," Oma

said as she picked up her large piece of cake and bit into it.

At the table, a few people stared, including Bradyn who mimicked Oma by picking up his own piece of cake. He shoved a huge bite into his mouth.

"You promised me you'd be on your best behavior," Klaude could hear Bennett say to Bradyn from the other end of the table. "I never should have invited you."

"That's not a nice thing to say," their father said.

They talked some more but Klaude tuned them out. He studied Oma's bite marks in her cake. As he guessed, the teeth marks were much larger than the teeth marks in his cake. Both the right front tooth mark and the left front tooth mark were clearly defined and some of her other teeth made frosting prints, too.

"You're the best, Oma," Klaude said. Whoever bit into Klaude's cake had something different going on with their left tooth. He had an idea of how he was going to solve the bite mark mystery.

It involved his grandmother and making people

laugh. "Will you do me another favor?" Klaude knew his grandmother was going to say yes even if his idea was crazy.

Chapter Five

Surprise Dance

Long before Klaude was born, Oma had been part of a German folk dance group. She still loved to dance, even if it was just with Klaude in the apartment living room or with the house plants.

Klaude asked Mrs. Holmes for permission so he wouldn't ruin her luncheon plans any more than he already had. "Sounds like a fun addition," she said. One of the cafeteria workers had a small music player and speakers. He even searched for the perfect song for Klaude.

Mrs. Holmes was so short that she had to lower the microphone to make the announcement. "We have a surprise as part of our luncheon celebration today—a special performance by Klaude and his grandmother!"

Klaude hoped this would be a good surprise and not a bad one.

The group of award winners, their family members, and the volunteers clapped as Klaude and Oma stepped on the cafeteria stage. Klaude's heart raced. Surely, he could've come up with a different solution that wasn't so embarrassing. Then again, he liked getting on stage and he loved making people laugh.

As polka music played over the small speakers in the cafeteria, Oma and Klaude took a spot center stage, close enough to the luncheon group to still get a good look.

Klaude and Oma had come up with their own version of the Chicken Dance and that's what they danced now in front of everyone. They started with a clap, clap, clap, and they shook their pretend tail feathers before Oma spun Klaude around. He nearly flew off the stage she spun him so quickly.

The audience laughed.

Klaude was almost too dizzy to study their faces and the shape of their teeth when everyone laughed again during the next round of clapping and tail feather shaking. Several of the younger kids in the audience danced along, including Bradyn.

Oma was a natural on stage. Klaude hammed it up to get more laughs——or "chickened" it up, rather. Too bad Klaude hadn't brought his recorder or else he might've put on another performance. Sure, he was having fun, but he also had a purpose. By the time the song ended Klaude made a couple of mental notes:

- Romy's right tooth stuck out slightly forward compared to his left tooth, which Klaude had never noticed before.
- Divya's right tooth overlapped her left tooth a little bit.
- Bradyn was missing his left front tooth.

Any one of those three could've been the cake biters. Romy was still upset about the food fight. Maybe Klaude had hurt Divya's feelings and she blamed him about the spaghetti mess. And Bradyn was a little kid who probably couldn't be trusted around cake.

"I had no idea you were going to dance," Romy said as he walked past Klaude to clear the plates away. The luncheon was ending soon. Oma went back to her spot at the table and this gave Klaude a good chance to find out if Romy was guilty.

"Hey, did my piece of cake taste good when you took a bite out of it?" Klaude asked.

Romy stopped walking and looked right at Klaude. Klaude had been right about Romy's teeth.

"Why in the world would I eat your cake when I got a slice of my own? Volunteers get to eat the same thing as the award winners. Why else do you think I asked to help out at the luncheon when I should've been one of the award winners instead?"

"Because it would give you a chance to pay me back for the food fight." Klaude paused a moment to think things through. Okay, fine, you didn't bite into my cake, but why did you put the plastic snake in my spaghetti, and why did you break my trophy?"

Romy shook his head. "I didn't break your trophy. I gotta go. Mrs. Holmes is waiting on me." Romy took off, walking much faster now.

A moment later, Bradyn begged to do a dance on stage, which Mrs. Holmes said would be fine. He got up there and shook his pretend tail feathers.

Klaude made his way back to the table slowly to inspect everyone's remaining cake bites. There wasn't much left over. The cake must've been delicious, not like Klaude knew anything about that. He didn't dare touch his cake after someone bit into it. Nurse Strongman was always getting on everyone's case at school about not spreading germs. Besides, who knows what might've been buried inside of it after the snake incident?

"You've got some funny moves," Bennett said when Klaude passed him by. "And so does my brother." Bradyn tried to do a handstand on stage but toppled over.

Klaude looked at the empty spot where Bradyn had been sitting and saw that the piece of cake he'd shoved into his mouth after watching Oma. It had the same exact bite mark as the one on his plate!

Chapter Six

One Mystery Down, Two to Go

Oma worried what Bradyn was going to be like after he ate sugar when the cake was being served, but what if he'd had some sugar beforehand? Klaude thought about the way Bradyn had run off behind the food counter, practically into the cafeteria kitchen. When Klaude talked to him after, he wiped something pink or red from his face. It could've been spaghetti sauce, but pink frosting seemed more likely.

"Your little brother is funny," Klaude said to Bennett in an attempt to waste a little time before Bradyn returned from the stage.

"He's a clown like you," Bennett said and then he tried to hide his face again. "Don't take that the wrong way because I wasn't trying to hurt your feelings or anything."

"I get it." Even if Klaude could tell that Bennett

got annoyed with his little brother, he also saw how protective he could be as well. Klaude needed to choose his words carefully when Bradyn returned from the cafeteria stage.

The little boy walked now instead of ran. Klaude figured his sugar rush might've been wearing off.

"You're a good dancer," Klaude told Bradyn.

Bradyn smiled. "Not as good as your grandma! She's awesome."

"Yeah, she is. Hey, I have a question. When you went behind the food counter, did you see any plates of cake?"

Bradyn nodded. "There were lots of them! Strawberry frosting—my favorite!"

Klaude leaned in to whisper. "Did you take a bite out of any of the slices?"

"You're not going to tell on me, are you?"

Klaude shook his head no. At this point, he just wanted answers to all of the luncheon mysteries.

"I took a bite out of one of the cakes. I might've eaten the whole thing but my brother caught me," Bradyn said.

Klaude could see that Bennett was trying to listen in. He whispered again, "Thanks for telling

me. Are you sure you didn't put a toy snake in my food?"

"I didn't. Promise."

"Did you break any trophy by accident?"

"No."

"Okay, then. Keep up the good dancing," Klaude said. He wanted to get back to Oma since he'd left her waiting for a little while.

"Wait!" Bradyn said, much louder. Bennett was staring at him. "I didn't tell you that you're a good dancer like your grandma."

Klaude smiled. Oma kept trying to enter him in a Centerville dance contest, but he didn't think he was good enough. Maybe he would sign up next time she mentioned it. Maybe there was even some kind of music contest. He was getting pretty good at playing the recorder.

Klaude thought it would be awesome if he could win a fancy trophy, not just a homemade school trophy with a painted golden spoon. He still hadn't figured out who broke it or why.

The toy snake was still a mystery too, but at least he knew who bit into his cake. Had someone delivered it to him on purpose, though?

When he sat back next to Oma, several of the third graders were talking to her and she was telling them all about her days traveling as a dancer. She smiled when she saw Klaude. "I got you a fresh piece of cake since it looked like someone started eating yours."

I have the best grandmother ever, he thought.

"Do you still dance in performances?" Divya

asked Oma.

"Only in my living room," she said.

Klaude was grateful she didn't mention anything about dancing in a bright orange leotard or that some of her dance partners were plants.

Maybe if Klaude signed up for the Centerville dance contests, Oma would sign up, too. There had to be all kinds of age groups. Oma was sure to win first place for the grandma age category.

Klaude had dealt with all kinds of issues during the luncheon, but maybe this was something good that would come out of it.

Chapter Seven

Klaude Searches for Answers

"You look nice," Klaude told Divya once the crowd around Oma broke up. "I feel bad about the mess, even if it wasn't my fault."

"It wasn't my fault either but I'm sorry I dumped the plate on you. At least I got to change into something clean," Divya said. "And I really like Queeneka's dress. She's got good style. You look nice, too. And well spiced."

"Ha, you're right. Did you know by any chance that you brought me a piece of cake with a bite out of it?"

Divya scrunched her face up in disgust. "Eww! I had no idea!"

Klaude filled her in on what happened and how Bradyn confessed. He was glad that Divya hadn't seen the cake and brought it out to him on purpose.

"That kid is trouble," Divya said. "I doubt he'll ever win a Golden Spoon Award when he gets old enough to go to Watson."

Klaude thought about how Oma said he was a lot like Bradyn at that age. "Who knows? Bradyn might win Most Improved Behavior someday."

Divya laughed even though Klaude hadn't tried to be funny. He liked when that happened. Sometimes, at least.

"By the way, before you served the spaghetti, did you see anyone else in the kitchen area that shouldn't have been there?"

Divya looked up at the cafeteria ceiling as if she was trying to find an answer written on it. That would've been awesome if ceiling tiles revealed answers. Klaude really wanted to resolve the two remaining mysteries.

"No," Divya answered.

Klaude was disappointed. The luncheon was wrapping up and he might never figure things out.

Oma whispered to Klaude, "She's a nice girl. I can tell that she'd make a great dancer."

Maybe Divya might enter the Centerville dance contest, too. It would be really cool if several kids from Watson Elementary School participated. They would have a good dance reputation as well as a reputation for being good detectives.

Mrs. Holmes went back to the microphone and thanked all of the families for attending the celebration. "Thanks to the cafeteria staff for making such a delicious meal! We here at Watson are so lucky for all of your hard work and dedication."

The audience clapped loudly. "Congratulations again to our award winners—keep up the great work! And last, but not least, thanks to our volunteers for helping this luncheon run mostly smoothly."

Divya waved and so did a couple of the other volunteers when the group cheered loudly. Romy bowed. When Klaude made eye contact with Romy, he looked away quickly.

Klaude couldn't forget Romy's smirk and his comment about the food fight. He also thought it was strange that Romy took off as fast as he did.

Sure, he denied breaking the trophy but he didn't mention anything about the plastic snake. He left that part out completely before stopping the conversation. Surely that was no accident.

The cafeteria workers might've slipped the toy snake into his food, but it made no sense why any of them would do that. They could get in serious trouble, especially if he happened to choke and die. Thankfully, neither one of those things happened. Besides, the cafeteria workers were the ones who had voted Klaude to win Most Improved Behavior.

Klaude needed to settle things with Romy once and for all.

Chapter Eight

A Confession or Two

"I'll be right back," Klaude told Oma. "Please don't leave until I get a chance to say goodbye."

"Of course not," Oma said, adjusting her dress. She had a small spaghetti sauce stain from hugging Klaude. He could see her wearing this dress later at a dance competition and he hoped that the stain would come out without any issues. Same for his outfit. The polo and pants were actually pretty comfortable compared to his normal jeans and T-shirt.

Romy saw Klaude coming to talk to him and he took off again.

"Romy, wait!" Bennett called.

Romy turned around when he heard Bennett's voice. Bennett handed him his jacket that he'd left on one of the chairs. Klaude caught up to Romy when he grabbed the jacket.

"It's not all that funny to me now, but you got me good with the snake," Klaude said.

Romy seemed like he couldn't help himself and he cracked a smile.

"I know you buried it in my spaghetti, so don't try denying it." Klaude tried to make a serious face even though he wanted to smile along with Romy.

"I about lost it when you yelled," Romy said, starting to laugh. "I wish I had a recording of how shocked you looked when you pulled the snake out of your mouth."

There it was—a confession! Klaude had now solved two of the three mysteries.

"How did you pull it off?" Klaude asked. It was a pretty decent prank. He liked to joke around better than he liked to pull pranks, but this knowledge might come in handy someday. Who knows?

"When the other volunteers started to grab the plates of food to pass out, I turned around and buried the snake under the top layer of spaghetti knowing that the plate was going to be delivered to you. I made sure of it." Romy started to laugh all over again.

"You're lucky I didn't choke or something."

Romy stopped laughing. "I didn't think that part through. I'm glad nothing bad happened."

"Nothing bad happened? I had a snake in my mouth!"

"At least it wasn't a real one. I borrowed my little brother's toy for today's occasion," Romy said. He must've been planning the prank for some time, probably since Mrs. Holmes made the announcement that Klaude had won the award and not him.

"Now will you finally get over the food fight thing?" Klaude asked. "I might've planted the idea in your mind, but I never made you throw that roll."

"I'll let it go as long as you don't tell Mrs. Holmes I was the one who put the snake in your meal," Romy said. "I'm holding out hope that I can get the Most Improved Behavior award next time."

"Deal!" Klaude said. The boys shook on it.

Klaude decided he would sign up as a volunteer at the next Good Manners Luncheon. He wasn't the type to prank, but the thought was tempting if Romy was up for an award. Really, Klaude just wanted a second chance at a yummy meal without everything going wrong.

The snake thing had been gross, but at least now Romy couldn't hold it over him any longer. To show that Klaude would hold up his end of the bargain, he returned the toy snake to Romy. It belonged to Romy's brother anyway.

******

"Why is my genius of a grandson looking so upset? Is he going to miss his dear old grandmother when she goes home?" Oma said at the end of the luncheon.

Klaude had to go back to class for the rest of the day and Oma would go back to the apartment to take care of the plants. Maybe she'd get a dance or two in with the peace lily. Even if he wasn't around, Klaude hoped she'd close the front curtains.

Klaude pointed to the broken Golden Spoon trophy Oma was carrying. "I solved the mystery about who put the toy snake in my food and who took a bite out of my cake, but I never did figure out what happened to the trophy."

Oma started choking. Klaude patted her on the

back, hoping she was okay. His grandmother was all he had and he needed her to be fine. Then he saw that she wasn't just choking, she was laughing.

"Oma? What's going on?"

His grandmother didn't speak for a moment and he tried to figure out why she was acting so strange. Then she explained. "I accidentally sat on it."

Klaude remembered how she cried out in pain when she first sat down at the luncheon. That must've been why! The trophy must've rolled off onto her chair before she sat down.

"I said 'I'm sorry' early but I didn't explain why," Oma said. "I didn't want to upset you on your special day. I plan to fix it with superglue just as I promised."

Klaude gave his grandmother a hug. "Thanks for all that you do for me."

Sure, the trophy would be better once Oma superglued it back together, but it would never be perfect. It would always be a reminder of this day, though. It was Klaude's first trophy, and he hoped it would be the first of many trophies to come.

How to Solve a Mystery
by Klaude

It was a surprise when I got voted for a Golden Spoon Award and got to attend the Good Manners Luncheon with Oma. Then I got some other surprises:

1 A toy snake in my spaghetti.
2 A broken trophy.
3 A bite out of my cake.

I considered who would've done this and why. Romy was a lead suspect since he was still mad at me after I kinda sorta encouraged him to start a food fight. He never got over it, especially since he got busted and I didn't, and then I won the award. Bradyn was a suspect since he was an out of control little kid who kept running all over the place. Divya might've done something too since she thinks I'm annoying. (So what? I like to joke around.)

After studying teeth marks, I figured out Bradyn bit into my cake. I gathered some clues and used what Romy said and, more importantly, what he didn't say to figure out he was the one who stuck the snake in my food. The broken trophy was a complete surprise to me. If I'd been paying more attention to the little details and suspected everyone, including my own grandmother, I might've been able to solve what happened. Good thing I talked to her!

Q & A with Author J. L. Anderson

How did you become interested in writing mysteries?
I loved reading mysteries when I was a girl and I was a big fan on Nancy Drew and the Hardy Boys. I write a variety of things for all kinds of ages, and I was drawn to writing mysteries because they're so fun to write. I really like thinking through the plots and planting red-herrings (false clues).

What was your greatest challenge writing this story?
I really love Klaude as a character and it was hard to think of ways to make him struggle. I had to think of several things that would happen to him that wouldn't be pleasant. When he figures things out, it felt even more rewarding to me because of his struggles.

Which character did you have the most fun creating?
Oma! She's a funny and interesting grandmother. I wish I knew her in real life!

Is there any connection between your real life and the story?
My husband's side of the family has German roots. My husband danced German folk dance when he was younger and he was the inspiration for this thread in the story.

Discussion Questions

1. List several ways that Klaude was misunderstood by his classmates.
2. What was another way that Klaude could've tried to see everyone's teeth?
3. What is one of your talents? Would you share your talents in front of your classmates? Why or why not?
4. Who did you suspect broke the trophy and why?

Vocabulary

Here is a list of some important words in
the story. Try to use the words in a sentence.
You can play a game of memory with the
vocabulary words. Write each word on a
separate card. Then write the definition on a
different set of cards. Mix up the cards and
place them face down on a flat surface. With
a partner, take turns flipping over two cards
each. If the cards make a pair, you get another
turn. The person with the most sets of cards
at the end of the game wins.

ceremony: a special event
confessed: admitted the truth
disappointed: upset, saddened
incident: event
inspect: checked
luncheon: a formal lunch
mayhem: chaos
mimicked: copycatted
realistic: lifelike

Vocabulary continued

shrieked: high pitched scream

suspect: a person thought to be guilty

teasing: mocking

trophy: a cup or decorated prize

Writing Prompt

Using one of the characters from the story as your main character, write a mystery about disappearing food in the lunchroom. Who is taking the food and why? How does the character solve the mystery?

Websites to Visit

Learn more about German folk dancing:
http://www.germanjuniorfolkdancers.ca

Play some detective games:
https://www.cia.gov/kids-page/games

Learn more about the German recorder:
http://gc-music.com/Recor.htm

About the Author

J. L. Anderson solves a mystery of her own almost every day like figuring out why her daughter is suddenly so quiet (what did she get into this time?), which of her two dogs stole the bag of treats, where her husband is taking her for a surprise dinner, or what happened to her keys this time. You can learn more about J.L. Anderson at www.jessicaleeanderson.com.

About the Illustrator

I have always loved drawing from a very young age. While I was at school, most of my time was spent drawing comics and copying my favorite characters. With  a portfolio under my arm, I started drawing comics for newspapers and fanzines. After I finished my studies I decided to try to make a living as a freelance illustrator... and here I am!